CALAMITY JANE
FRONTIERSWOMAN

Retold by
ALICIA Z. KLEPEIS

Illustrated by
MATÍAS LAPEGÜE

Cavendish Square

New York

THERE ONCE WAS A GIRL NAMED MARTHA JANE Cannary. She was born in a cabin on a farm in Missouri in 1852. When she was young, her friends and family called her Marthy. When she grew up, she became known as Calamity Jane.

Marthy often had to do chores on her family's farm. She also had to help look after her five younger brothers and sisters. But Marthy was not happy just doing this work. She was not like most other girls. A neighbor even said Marthy was wild like a lynx kitten!

Marthy loved being outdoors. She started riding horses at an early age. She quickly became an expert rider. She could ride even the most stubborn or wild horses.

Out in the countryside, Marthy longed for adventure. When she was about twelve years old, she got her wish. Her parents decided to move from Missouri to Montana. How exciting!

On a spring day in 1865, the Cannary family started their five-month journey. Hoping to avoid attack by Native Americans, they joined other folks traveling west. Their group formed a wagon train.

Marthy did not like wearing her full skirt, so she borrowed boys' trousers. She even rode astride her horse rather than side-saddle. This was not how ladies back then were supposed to behave. She didn't want to sit in the wagon or walk alongside the oxen. Instead, Marthy spent almost all her time with the men. She hunted animals and swam across streams. She proved that she could shoot a gun just like the men.

Finally, the Cannary family arrived at a Montana mining camp called Virginia City. But luck was not on their side. Not long after their big journey, both of Marthy's parents died.

Looking for excitement, Marthy moved on. She headed to Wyoming. At times, she would cook or wash clothes to make money, but these jobs bored her. Marthy decided to try something unusual. She dressed in men's work clothes. That way, no one would know who she really was.

In Wyoming, Marthy met some men who were helping to build the nation's railroads. She was hired as a bullwhacker, or someone who drives teams of oxen. The oxen pulled wagons that carried everything the workers needed, from railroad tools to potatoes. Marthy realized she could make a lot of money as a bullwhacker. Always one to brag, she said she could "pick a fly off [an] oxen's ear four times out of five." She loved telling the workmen stories after a long day's work. She chatted with them over coffee, bacon, and bread.

Bullwhacking was not Marthy's only job in Wyoming. She also worked as a scout for the US Army. It was during her scout days that many say Martha Jane Cannary earned her nickname Calamity Jane.

As one story says, one day, Marthy and some soldiers were on their way back to their camp. Suddenly, they were attacked by a big group of Sioux Native Americans.

Right in front of her, Marthy saw another soldier, Captain Egan, get shot. Being a strong woman, she lifted the wounded man onto her horse. Then she took him to a nearby fort. Once he recovered, Captain Egan said, "I name you Calamity Jane, the heroine of the plains."

Calamity Jane loved her new name. Each time she arrived in a new town, she enjoyed swinging open the doors to a saloon and shouting, "I'm Calamity Jane!" She was the only woman in such places. Dressed as a man, she would tell tales and have a good time with all the other men. She was pretty friendly, but sometimes she got into trouble for being too rowdy.

Calamity Jane never backed down from a challenge. She was fast as lightning on her horse, and she wasn't afraid of anything. She raced to deliver messages between US Cavalry camps in Wyoming. Sometimes she had to swim across a river and then ride many miles while chilly and wet. Still, she got the messages where they needed to go.

One time, though, on her long ride to Fort Fetterman, Calamity Jane caught a cold after crossing a river. She ended up in the hospital.

Nothing kept Calamity Jane down for long, though. Once she got back on her feet, she moved on. This time, she headed to Fort Laramie. There she met a scout named William Hickok, known to many as Wild Bill Hickok. Calamity Jane enjoyed his company. When news of gold in the Dakota Territory arrived, Calamity Jane and Wild Bill wasted no time. Yee-haw! They were off!

Calamity Jane, Wild Bill, and their friends had lots of adventures on the two-week trip from Fort Laramie to the Black Hills. The men admired Calamity Jane's bullwhacking skills. Her talents came in handy.

One day, the group saw a coyote in the distance. The men fired at it with their rifles and missed. Then Calamity Jane tried. Joseph White-Eye Anderson said Calamity Jane killed that coyote "with a six-shooter when it was over one hundred yards away."

This group caused quite a scene riding into Deadwood, South Dakota. They paraded down Main Street wearing buckskin suits with lots of fringe. One night, while they were celebrating in a saloon, the owner asked Calamity Jane to quiet down. She did not like being told what to do, so she aimed her gun at a mirror and shot it. The mirror shattered into many pieces. Calamity Jane made it clear that no one told her what to do or how to behave.

Calamity Jane thought Wild Bill was handsome. She liked his big moustache and the way he dressed. She even told people that they were married.

Not long after arriving in Deadwood, a criminal named Jack McCall shot and killed Wild Bill during a card game. When she heard the news, Calamity Jane was shocked.

There was lots of crime in the Wild West, but Calamity Jane was brave. One morning, she was out riding her horse, not far from Deadwood. Up ahead, she saw a stagecoach coming. But something was wrong. There was no driver! Native Americans were chasing the coach.

Calamity Jane caught up with the horses and took control. Then she hurried to Deadwood to deliver its passengers and goods safely.

In 1878, a terrible disease called smallpox struck Deadwood. There was no cure for it. Most people were afraid to look after the sick—but not Calamity Jane. She cared for them over many weeks. One story says that one day, the local doctor found Calamity Jane taking care of sick miners. "You just tell me what to do, Doc, and I'll do it," she said.

When Calamity Jane needed supplies for the sick miners, her fierce side kicked in. One day, she went to a nearby general store and filled a sack with food, but she did not want to pay. When the storekeeper told her how much she owed, Calamity Jane drew her gun and backed out the door. After this episode, other merchants offered free blankets and food to the smallpox victims. Not all of Calamity Jane's patients lived, though. She buried the men who didn't survive.

Calamity Jane changed her mind a lot. She also changed where and with whom she lived. She married several different men during her life. For a while, she'd say her last name was Somers or Dorsett or Hunt or Dalton or Burke, but none of these husbands lasted very long. Calamity Jane was restless. She always moved on.

After the smallpox outbreak, Calamity Jane looked for gold. Then she went to Rapid City, South Dakota, and took a job as a bullwhacker. Traveling between Rapid City and Fort Pierre, she kept her oxen in line. She braved the dust when it was dry. She plodded through muddy rivers. She cracked her rawhide whip to keep the oxen moving.

When she was older, Calamity Jane put on a fringed suit and fancy leather boots and joined a show run by her friend Buffalo Bill Cody. She performed around the country, from Minneapolis to Buffalo. She told the tales of her adventures. She greeted the crowds. She wrote a book and sold copies of her autobiography. But she preferred telling stories with friends.

After a few years, she no longer liked living in cities. Calamity Jane asked Buffalo Bill to give her the money for a train ticket home. He agreed.

Calamity Jane headed back to the West. She spent her last days enjoying time with her friends. She died at the age of forty-seven.

During her lifetime, Calamity Jane did jobs no other woman had done before. She proved that women could shoot, drive oxen, and make a living as well as any men of the time. She never gave up!

ABOUT THE LEGEND

It is known that Calamity Jane was an expert sharpshooter and horsewoman, but accurate, detailed information about her isn't always available. Some has been lost over time.

Many historians believe that while some of the stories about Martha Jane Cannary are true, many of them are not. In fact, many of the dates, places, and events she talked about do not check out with historical or government documents. Calamity Jane often exaggerated things when telling her life story.

It is really difficult to say for sure what about Calamity Jane's life is fact and what is legend, since so many versions of her stories have been told through the generations.

WORDS TO KNOW

astride Riding a horse with one leg on each side of the horse's back.

autobiography The story of a person's life written by the person herself.

rowdy Loud or rough in behavior.

saloon A place of business where alcoholic drinks are sold.

scout A person sent to gather information, especially to prepare for military action.

TO FIND OUT MORE

BOOKS

Brimner, Larry D. *Calamity Jane*. Tall Tales. North Mankato, MN: Compass Point Books, 2004.

Krensky, Stephen. *Calamity Jane*. On My Own Folklore. Minneapolis, MN: Millbrook Press, Inc., 2007.

Sanford, William R., and Carl R. Green. *Calamity Jane: Courageous Wild West Woman*. Courageous Heroes of the American West. Berkeley Heights, NJ: Enslow Publishers, Inc., 2012.

WEBSITES

History: Calamity Jane Is Born

http://www.history.com/this-day-in-history/calamity-jane-is-born

This is the link to an article that gives information about the life of Calamity Jane.

The Legend of Calamity Jane, "A Slip of the Whip"

http://www.youtube.com/watch?v=vxj654C2kps

This cartoon tells a story about Calamity Jane and her seeking out justice on the plains.

ABOUT THE AUTHOR

Alicia Z. Klepeis began her career at the National Geographic Society. She is the author of many kids' books, including *The World's Strangest Foods, Bizarre Things We've Called Medicine, Francisco's Kites,* and *From Pizza to Pisa.* She lives with her family in upstate New York.

ABOUT THE ILLUSTRATOR

Matías Lapegüe was born in Buenos Aires, Argentina, in 1977. As a child, he enjoyed drawing animations from science fiction movies. As a teenager, he dedicated his time to sports. Later on he fell in love again with drawing. He graduated with a degree in graphic design in 2004 and worked as a freelancer both in graphic and web design. Lapegüe studied digital color with Nestor Pereyra, a well-respected colorist. He is currently creating new worlds and characters for young and old alike.

Published in 2017 by Cavendish Square Publishing, LLC
243 5th Avenue, Suite 136, New York, NY 10016

First Edition

Website: cavendishsq.com

This publication represents the opinions and views of the author based on his or her personal experience, knowledge, and research. The information in this book serves as a general guide only. The author and publisher have used their best efforts in preparing this book and disclaim liability rising directly or indirectly from the use and application of this book.

CPSIA Compliance Information: Batch #CW17CSQ

All websites were available and accurate when this book was sent to press.

Cataloging-in-Publication Data

Names: Klepeis, Alicia Z.
Title: Calamity Jane: frontierswoman / Alicia Z. Klepeis.
Description: New York : Cavendish Square Publishing, 2017. |
Series: American legends and folktales | Includes index.
Identifiers: ISBN 9781502622006 (pbk.) | ISBN 9781502622020 (library bound) |
ISBN 9781502622013 (6 pack) | ISBN 9781502622051 (ebook)
Subjects: LCSH: Calamity Jane, 1856-1903--Juvenile fiction. |
Women pioneers--West (U.S.)--Juvenile literature. | Pioneers--West (U.S.)--Juvenile literature.
Classification: LCC PZ7.K55 Ca 2017 | DDC [F]--dc23

Editorial Director: David McNamara
Editor: Kristen Susienka
Copy Editor: Nathan Heidelberger
Associate Art Director: Amy Greenan
Designer: Alan Sliwinski
Illustrator: Matías Lapegüe
Production Coordinator: Karol Szymczuk

Printed in the United States of America